Piers

Finds his Voice

First published in the United Kingdom in 2005
by Chrysalis Children's Books,
an imprint of Chrysalis Books Group plc
The Chrysalis Building
Bramley Road
London W10 6SP
www.chrysalisbooks.co.uk

This book was created for Chrysalis Children's Books by Zuza Books.
Text and illustrations copyright © Zuza Books

Zuza Vrbova asserts her moral right to be
identified as the author of this work.
Tom Morgan-Jones asserts his moral right to be
identified as the illustrator of this work.

BRITISH LIBRARY CATALOGUING-IN-PUBLICATION DATA
A catalogue record for this book is available from the British Library.

ISBN 1 84458 406 2

Printed in China
2 4 6 8 10 9 7 5 3 1

Piers
Finds his Voice

Zuza Vrbova

Illustrated by Tom Morgan-Jones

CHRYSALIS CHILDREN'S BOOKS

Every day at school, Piers sat at the same desk
by the window. He liked to stare out of the window
and daydream about home.

Every day, Miss Roo called out the name of everyone
in the class, in alphabetical order. When she got to
the letter P, the same thing always happened.

"Piers?" she called out.

Piers didn't say anything. Piers never said anything.

Piers liked to speak in his own language.
On his way to school, Piers always chatted
non-stop to his sister, Penny.

6

"Will you meet me at lunchtime?" Piers always asked,
looking worried.

"Of course," said Penny. "Let's meet under the big oak tree."
And they linked arms.

Piers liked to write stories. He wrote long stories about where he came from.

Miss Roo always wrote, 'Very good, Piers!' at the end of each story.

But Piers knew Miss Roo didn't understand his stories. They were written in a language she didn't know.

8

One day, Miss Roo asked Piers to read out loud.
But Piers just stared at the book.

After a long silence, he began to talk about
the pictures. But as he spoke in his own language,
no one understood what he was saying.

Tabby liked reading out loud.
She took over, "Today's story is
about a wolf called White Fang.
White Fang was born in
the snow. His father was
a dog and his mother
was a wolf."

Then Tabby read the book out loud.

    Piers listened to the words. They sounded
very strange to him. He couldn't understand the story,
but he liked the pictures. They reminded him of home.

At playtime, Pamela said to Piers, "Come and play football!"

Pamela looked friendly and Piers wanted to say
something to her. But he didn't.

Then Misty asked, "Why don't you come and climb
on the climbing frame?"

Piers just looked at her. He wished he was back home.

Then he noticed Bridget playing hopscotch by herself.

I know how to play that! Piers thought.

He went a bit closer to Bridget. Bridget didn't say anything.

She just smiled, and they played hopscotch together.

At lunchtime, Piers went to the oak tree.

Penny was there, waiting for him.

"What's the matter, Piers?" Penny asked.

"I can't really understand what everyone is saying.

Let's just speak our own language," said Piers.

16

"Eh-ah," said Penny, which meant 'yes'.

"Promise?" asked Piers.

"Promise."

And they linked arms.

17

The next day, when Miss Roo called out everyone's name, everyone answered, "Yes."

But when Miss Roo called out, "Piers?" he answered, "Eh-ah."

Everyone laughed. Crispin laughed so hard
that he fell off his seat.

"Now, let's do some drawing," said Miss Roo,
trying to calm down the class.

Rudy drew a big carrot. Then he felt hungry,
but he didn't know why. Both the twins copied Rudy
and drew a carrot too. Their carrots were identical —
just like the twins themselves.

Piers stared out of the window for a long time.
After a while, he picked up a coloured pencil and
started to draw. He drew a picture of his home.

Piers's home was round. It was surrounded by fir trees.
There was lots of snow. In front of his home, he drew
a big red tricycle – the one that he had left behind.

The more Piers looked at his picture, the sadder he felt.

"Very good, Piers," said Miss Roo, wondering how
to cheer him up.

Even in the summer, Piers wore his red woolly hat
to school. Piers didn't say anything, except "eh-ah".
He didn't play with anyone, except Bridget.
(They became very good at hopscotch.)

Piers and Penny met every day at lunchtime
and told each other everything.

25

One day, Miss Roo said, "Today, we have a special treat. We are going to watch a film."

"Hooray!" everyone shouted.

Miss Roo had chosen a film about Piers's home. Everyone in it looked just like Piers. They all said "eh-ah" – just like Piers did. All the houses were round and surrounded by fir trees. And there was lots of snow everywhere.

"That's my home!" shouted Piers.

Everyone looked at Piers. He could speak their language! He just didn't know he could. Everyone clapped and cheered.

"Hurray for Piers!" they shouted.

Piers blushed. He wasn't used to so much attention. But for once, he was happy.

After the film, everyone had lots
of questions for Piers. Piers talked a lot.
He had never talked so much in his life.
Miss Roo even called him a chatterbox!

Later that day, Piers told Penny,

"Maybe this language is not so bad."

"And after all," said Penny,

"we can always speak both."

And they linked arms and went home.